RAGGEDY ANN AND ANDY AND
THE HAUNTED DOLL HOUSE

by Jane E. Gerver
pictures by Carol Nicklaus

RAGGEDY ANN AND ANDY AND

THE HAUNTED DOLL HOUSE

It was nighttime. The toys and dolls sat on the playroom shelves. Raggedy Ann and Andy were tucked in their beds. Marcella was fast asleep in her room next door.

035302

Suddenly there were heavy footsteps outside the playroom.

"Someone's coming!" whispered Raggedy Ann. "Shh!" All the others were very quiet. They didn't want anyone to know that they could talk.

The playroom door opened, and in came
Marcella's mother and father. They were carrying
a big package wrapped in beautiful gift paper.

"Let's put it over there," said Marcella's
mother. They placed the package in a corner of
the room, and then tiptoed out.

"What do you think it is?" asked Raggedy Andy.

"Maybe it's a present for Marcella," said Raggedy Ann.

The Rocking Horse pricked up his ears. "I hear a noise coming from the package," he said.

The dolls listened carefully. They could hear faint creakings and a rattle coming from the package.

"I don't like strange sounds!" said the pretty French doll.

"We'll just have to wait until tomorrow to find out what they are," Raggedy Ann said to the others.

The next morning, as soon as Marcella opened her eyes, she knew it was a special day. It was her birthday!

She ran into the playroom. The gaily-wrapped package was in the corner. Marcella unwrapped it — and found a beautiful doll house! A family of four little dolls — a mother, a father, and two children — sat in the front parlor.

"Oh, it's just what I wanted!" cried Marcella.

Raggedy Ann and Raggedy Andy gave each other a wink of their shoe-button eyes. They were glad the birthday present made Marcella so happy.

Marcella played with the doll house all day.

When bedtime came, she put the new little dolls in their very own beds. Then she went to bed herself.

Now it was safe for the toys and dolls in the playroom to speak.

"Marcella didn't ride on me at all today," complained the Rocking Horse.

Jack-in-the-Box bobbed his head up and down. "She didn't play with me, either!"

"One would think that Miss Marcella had forgotten all about us," sniffed the French doll. She shook her head and her blonde curls bounced.

"Now, now," said Raggedy Ann. "I'm sure Marcella will play with us again."

"And we should be friendly to the new dolls," said Raggedy Andy. "Let's ask them to join in our fun tonight. They must be feeling very lonely."

Raggedy Ann agreed with her brother. "I will go with you, Andy," she said.

As the Raggedies neared the doll house, they heard the strange sounds again.

Creak! Creak!

"What — what's that?" whispered Raggedy Andy. He felt a little nervous.

"A creaking sound," said Raggedy Ann. She was a sensible doll. "And it's coming from the doll house, just like last night."

"Look at that!" said Andy, pointing toward the windows. The shutters were swinging back and forth.

"How very strange," Raggedy Ann said. "Why would the shutters move like that? There's no wind in the playroom."

Then they saw a white figure peering out of a window. It disappeared — and reappeared on the floor above!

"You're smart, Ann," quavered Andy. "What would you call that thing in the window?"

"A ghost," said Raggedy Ann firmly.

"I don't like ghosts!" said Raggedy Andy. "This house is haunted!"

Raggedy Ann was scared too. But she said, "If we're scared, Andy, then just think how the dolls in the house must feel! We must help them."

She knocked on the door. *Thump, thump.* But there was no answer.

"Hello," she called softly. "It's us, Raggedy Ann and Andy. We want to help you." Still there was no answer.

Andy put his ear to the house. Then he heard the frightened voices of the dolls inside the house.

"Go away! Leave us alone!" they cried.

"Maybe they're scared of us," said Raggedy Andy. "After all, we're much bigger than they are."

"I have an idea," said Raggedy Ann. "With my magic wishing pebble, we can make ourselves small. Then perhaps they'll let us into the house."

Raggedy Ann's wishing pebble was hidden deep inside her cotton stuffing. Standing side by side, she and Raggedy Andy said, "We wish to be small enough to fit in the doll house."

Poof! In an instant, they had both shrunk to a few inches high.

This time, Mr. Doll opened the door when Raggedy Ann knocked.

"We want to welcome you to the playroom," said Raggedy Andy.

"Thank you," said Mr. Doll politely. "Won't you come in?"

The two Raggedies followed him into the parlor. Mrs. Doll and the children were huddled together, and they jumped when they saw Raggedy Ann and Raggedy Andy standing in the doorway.

"Please don't be scared of us!" said Raggedy Ann. "We're here to help you."

"We saw a ghost in the window and heard creaking noises!" said Raggedy Andy. "Is your house haunted?"

The doll family nodded. "We think it is," said Mrs. Doll. "but we don't know why — except that it is a very old house."

"We used to live in a box in the toystore," said Mr. Doll. "We only moved into this house yesterday," he added. "And then we found this piece of paper." He gave the the paper to Raggedy Ann, who read the scribbly writing on it aloud.

"Special words
Will banish the spell,
Use them wisely
And all will be well."

"Hmm," said Raggedy Andy. "The only special word I know is 'abracadabra.'"

But nothing special happened.

"How about 'shazam'?" suggested Raggedy Ann. Suddenly there was a loud creak from upstairs.

"Can you really banish the spell?" asked Mrs. Doll anxiously.

"We can try," said Raggedy Andy. He was starting to feel brave. "I think we should explore the house."

The two rag dolls walked through the doll house, room by room.

The creaking sounds grew louder on the second floor. Ann and Andy searched all the bedrooms, but they didn't find anything strange.

"Only the attic is left," Raggedy Andy said to Ann. Up the attic stairs they went, step by step.

And then —

"Boo!" shouted someone from behind the attic door. Ann and Andy gasped in surprise.

A little doll, clutching a broom and wearing a pointed hat, jumped out at them.

"Who — who are you?" asked Raggedy Ann.

'I'm a witch, of course," said the doll. "See my broom? And my hat?"

"Did you cast a spell on this house?" demanded Andy.

The witch frowned. "Yes, I did," she said.

"But why?" asked the Raggedies.

"Because this used to be *my* house," said the witch. "That is, before the new family moved in."

The other dolls crowded into the attic. "Why do you want to dress up like a ghost and scare other dolls?" asked Mr. Doll.

"I'm lonely!" the witch burst out. "Besides, the only thing I know how to do is cast spells and haunt houses."

"It's no fun being lonely," said Mrs. Doll. "Let's be friends. Then you won't have to haunt our house anymore."

The little witch gave the other dolls a shy smile. "It's not all that much fun being a witch," she confessed. "I'd rather try being a friend."

"And you don't have to be lonely, either, Mr. and Mrs. Doll," said Raggedy Ann. "All the dolls and toys in the playroom would like to meet you!"

"Come join us in our fun tonight!" said Raggedy Andy.

So all the little dolls followed Ann and Andy across the playroom. The other toys were waiting by the toyshelf, and sent up a cheer when they saw the doll-house family.

Then Raggedy Ann used her magic wishing pebble again. She and Andy grew to their proper size.

"Please play with us!" said Jack-in-the-Box to the little dolls.

"Let me give you all a ride!" said the Rocking Horse.

Soon the new dolls were merrily dancing and playing.

"Raggedy Ann," whispered Andy, "I still don't understand exactly what we did to banish the spell from the doll house."

"Well," said Raggedy Ann, who had been thinking the same thing to herself, "I think the real magic is in the special words 'Let's be friends.'"

And as usual, she was right!